Feel Good
Fairy Cakes

Look out for more

Bake a Wish

books:

Can-Do Crispies

Get-Better Jelly

Feel Fearless Flapjacks

Bake a Wish

Feel Good Fairy Cakes

Lorna Honeywell

Illustrated by Samantha Chaffey

MSCHOLASTIC

With special thanks to Pearl Morrison

First published in the UK in 2012 by Scholastic Children's Books
An imprint of Scholastic Ltd
Euston House, 24 Eversholt Street
London, NW1 1DB, UK
Registered office: Westfield Road, Southam, Warwickshire, CV47 0RA
SCHOLASTIC and associated logos are trademarks and/
or registered trademarks of Scholastic Inc.

ISBN 978 1 407 13113 9

A CIP catalogue record for this book is available from the British Library.

Typeset by M Rules
Printed and bound by CPI Group (UK) Ltd, Croydon, CR0 4YY

Papers used by Scholastic Children's Books are made
from wood grown in sustainable forests.

1 3 5 7 9 10 8 6 4 2

www.scholastic.co.uk/zone

A Bad Case of the Grumps

Lily Dalton rushed out of her classroom as fast as she could. She had got a gold star for her English homework and she couldn't wait to tell Grandma!

As she ran out into the playground, she looked round for the bright red coat that Grandma always wore. Lily grinned as she spotted her waiting with Lily's little brother, Archie, by the willow tree.

Today Grandma was looking extra colourful because she was wearing her red

coat *and* her blue shoes, and she had a
flowered scarf wrapped round her shoulders.

Grandma waved as she saw Lily, but Archie didn't. Archie was only four and his nursery always ended earlier than Lily's primary school. But both of them finished before Mum and Dad got home from work, so they always went back to Grandma's house after school and stayed with her and Grandpa until Mum or Dad came to pick them up.

Archie looked just like Lily. They had the same brown, wavy hair, although Lily's was long and Archie's was short, and they both had chocolate-brown eyes and dimples in their cheeks when they smiled.

But Archie wasn't smiling now. In fact, he didn't look very happy at all, Lily thought as she hurried over to them.

"Hi, Grandma!" she grinned, reaching up for a hug. "Hi, Archie!" Lily tried to hug him too, but Archie just crossed his arms sulkily.

"How was school today, Lilybee?" Grandma asked.

Lily's smile grew even wider. "Miss Peters gave me a gold star!"

Grandma was so pleased that she gave Lily another hug. "Oh, well done!" she smiled.

"Can I have a lucky dip?" Lily asked. "Please!"

Grandma pretended to think about it for a minute. "Ooh, yes, I think so."

Lily dipped her hand in Grandma's coat

 pocket. There were always some kinds of tasty sweets and treats in there. You never knew what you would find! Lily brought out a toffee

in a shiny wrapper.

"Do you want a sweetie, Archie?" Grandma asked, but he just scowled and turned his head away. "Oh dear." Grandma made a worried face at Lily over Archie's head. "I don't think you've had quite such a good day, have you?"

Archie shook his head and stuck his bottom lip out in a sulky pout.

"Come on, then," Grandma said as she took his hand. "Let's go home."

Grandpa was digging in the vegetable patch when they walked through the back garden. He pushed his hat back from his face and gave a big welcoming smile. "Why, hello, Lily. Hello, Archie. How was school today?"

Lily rushed over and told him about her gold star. Grandpa picked her up and swung her round.

"We have a genius in the family!" he joked as she squealed happily. Then he saw Archie's grumpy face. "Why don't you put your wellies on and come in the garden, Archie? I just saw a worm in the cabbage patch." Grandpa stretched his arms wide. "It was thi-i-s big."

Lily knew Archie loved being in the garden with Grandpa, especially if there were really big worms around. But Archie just shook his head and marched into the house.

"Oh, dear," Grandpa said. "Somebody's not in a very good mood."

"I know," Lily whispered. "He's been like this all the way home."

"Well, I hope he cheers up soon," Grandpa said, as he went back to his digging.

Lily followed Archie and Grandma into

the kitchen. She watched as Archie pulled off his shoes and dropped his bag on the floor. He walked right past Grandma's ginger-striped cat, Hector, who was lying on the kitchen window sill, enjoying the warm sunshine pouring in through the window.

Hector jumped down when he saw Archie and purred loudly, ready for the

tummy rub Archie usually gave him, but Archie didn't even look at him. Now Lily knew there was something *seriously* wrong.

Grandma sat down and

pulled Archie up on to her lap. Lily sat on the floor at their feet and gave Hector a nice stroke.

"Now then," Grandma said to Archie. "Why don't you tell me what's wrong and let's see if we can make it better."

Archie's bottom lip wobbled, and his voice was so quiet that Grandma and Lily had to lean in close to hear him. "I lost my pen." He sniffed and looked at Lily with big tears in his eyes. "My dinosaur one."

"I'm sure it's around somewhere," Lily comforted him.

But Archie wasn't finished yet. "And Miss Dawn wasn't at school so we had to do extra *numbers*. I can't do numbers! I *hate* them."

"Oh dear," said Grandma. "You *have* had a bad day." She stroked his hair gently. "But Miss Dawn will probably be back tomorrow and we can ask Mummy and Daddy about the pen. So let's cheer up. What would you like to do this afternoon?"

"Nothing." Archie declared. "I'm too sad."

Lily sighed. She hated seeing her little brother so gloomy. "Isn't there anything we can do to cheer him up, Grandma?" she asked. "Something really special?"

Grandma looked like she was thinking very hard. "Hmmm. . ." She glanced at Lily and then at Archie. His bottom lip was pouting as far as it could go. "This is the *worst* case of the grumps I've ever seen!" Grandma declared. "Something has to be done." She turned to the old cat lying stretched out on the floor. "Do you think it's time, Hector?"

Hector raised his head and purred.

Lily was curious and a little excited too. She wound her hair round and round her finger. "Time for what, Grandma?"

Grandma clapped her hands and smiled.

"Hector and I know just the thing to cheer Archie up!" Archie scrambled off her lap as she stood up and walked over to the large dresser where she kept her best plates and china teapots.

Lily and Archie watched as Grandma stood on her tiptoes to reach the top shelf. Hector was watching her too. He gave a soft meow as Grandma lifted down a large white jar decorated with yellow stripes.

As Grandma gently put the jar on the table, the kitchen felt very still for a moment. Then Hector leapt on to a chair at the table. At the same time, a sudden breeze blew in through the open window, making Lily's skirt flutter, and the old cuckoo clock on the wall began to sound.

"Cuckoo! Cuckoo!" the wooden bird sang four times before disappearing back inside the clock.

"What's happening?" Archie asked.

Grandma smiled and tapped the jar. "I'm going to show you something very special."

Archie went over to the table and Lily helped him climb up into his seat. "A jar?" Archie frowned.

"Ah, but not an *ordinary* jar," Grandma told him.

Lily's stomach hopped with excitement. "Is there something good inside it?"

Grandma gave a secret smile and nodded. "*Magic*," she whispered.

Lily's eyes opened as wide as they could go. "Magic?"

Archie was suddenly a lot more interested. He knelt up on his chair and stared at the jar. "What's magic about it?"

Grandma put her hand on the lid. "First we need to make a wish," she smiled. "Hmmm, what shall we wish for?"

"An elephant?" Archie suggested.

"We could do, but I don't think it'd fit in the kitchen." Grandma chuckled. "What about something that we really need?"

"I know!" Lily exclaimed. "Let's wish that Archie's bad mood goes away!"

"Yes," Archie grumbled. "I don't like being cross."

"Good idea, Lily!" Grandma smiled.

Lily closed her eyes and put her hands on the cool pottery. The jar felt smooth under her fingers. "I wish that Archie's bad mood goes away," she whispered.

"I wish my mood goes away." Archie mumbled. "And that I could do my numbers," he added quickly.

"Can we look inside?" Lily asked, jumping up and down with excitement.

"Are you sure you're ready to open it?" Grandma teased.

"Yes!" Archie and Lily shouted together.

Sunlight glinted off a vase on the window sill, filling the kitchen with rainbows. Lily and Archie gasped with excitement as she carefully opened the jar. As she pulled off the lid, she smiled. "Let the magic begin."

Grandma's Yummy Cupboard

Lily and Archie squeezed close together and stared at the open jar. Lily wondered what the magic might do. She loved reading books about fairies, but she never thought that there would be real, live magic in Grandma's kitchen!

"Look inside," Grandma smiled. Archie leant back a bit nervously. Lily peeked in to the jar.

"What can you see?" he asked.

"Chocolate chips!" Lily exclaimed. "And

some little cake cases. Oh! And a piece of rolled-up paper."

Grandma put her hand into the jar and took out the paper. "Would you read it for us, Lily?"

Lily uncurled the paper carefully.

Archie moved a little closer. "Is it a spell?" he asked. "In my cartoon a wizard said a spell that went KA-BOOM!"

Lily shook her head as she looked at it. There was a list of ingredients and directions for cooking. "Oh! It's a recipe!" she cried. "But it doesn't say what it makes," she said, passing it to Grandma.

"Ah ha!" Grandma read the recipe and her eyes twinkled. "Well, isn't that lucky? This is a recipe for Feel Good Fairy Cakes! Anyone who eats them will instantly feel in a good mood."

Lily gasped. "But how did it get into the jar?"

Grandma shrugged her shoulders. "Magic!" she grinned. "The jar will always give us just the recipe we need to make our wish come true."

"So it'll fix Archie's bad mood?" Lily asked.

"*Most definitely*," Grandma said, nodding her head firmly.

"Oh good!" Lily smiled. "You hear that, Archie? You can eat one and then you won't be in a bad mood any more!"

Archie smiled at that. He knelt up on his chair and looked into the jar. "But where are the fairy cakes?" he moaned.

"We're going to follow the recipe and

bake them," Grandma told him. "A recipe is like a spell, Archie. It turns lots of different ingredients into something extra yummy. But you have to help make the magic happen."

"But it'll take ages!" Archie complained.

"Come on, Archie, it'll be fun," Lily grinned. "We're making a real magic potion!" Lily wiggled her fingers and cackled like a witch, but Archie didn't even smile.

Grandma took the cake cases and the chocolate chips out of the jar and rolled up her sleeves. "Lily, why don't you go and fetch aprons for you and Archie to wear?"

Lily rushed to where Grandma's aprons were hanging on a hook behind the kitchen door. She'd eaten the yummy cakes and biscuits Grandma baked, but she'd never helped her make them . . . and now she was baking something *magical*! If they started making the fairy cakes now, then they should be ready before Mum and Dad picked them up.

While Lily put on a pretty apron covered with big red flowers, Grandma helped Archie into a blue and white stripy one and tied it for him. It was much too big, and Archie looked funny with the apron trailing down to his toes. Lily giggled. Archie pouted.

"Hmm, maybe I'll have to find you some aprons of your own for next time," Grandma smiled.

"One with dinosaurs on?" Archie asked hopefully.

"Perhaps." Grandma turned on the oven. "Now, whenever we do any cooking,

the first thing we have to do is wash our hands. And the second thing we do is put some music on!" She laughed, turning a knob on the radio so that the kitchen was filled with the happy music Grandma always listened to.

Lily and Archie rushed over to the kitchen sink. Once their hands were clean, Grandma showed them the larder where she kept her baking ingredients. It was a large cupboard, big enough for Lily and Archie to stand inside.

Lily looked up in wonder. Every shelf was full of jars and bottles, bags and packets. Lily could see cake decorations, birthday candles, marzipan and icing. Best of all, the cupboard smelled amazing!

Her nose twitched as she breathed in the sweet scent. "I can smell toasted marshmallows!" she giggled.

Archie licked his lips. "I can smell
popcorn . . . and jelly and . . . um . . .
chocolate."

"I'm going to call this the Yummy Cupboard," Lily smiled.

Grandma laughed. "Why don't I read out the recipe and you two can bring the ingredients over to the table?"

Lily was so excited she started bouncing on the spot. She and Archie were so lucky. They had the best grandma in the world. She was as cuddly as a koala bear, was never, ever grumpy *and* she had a magic cooking jar!

Grandma began reading from the recipe. "First, we need self-raising flour. That's what makes the cakes grow when you cook them. It's in a blue and white paper bag."

"I'll get it!" Archie said. But the flour was too high for him to reach. He jumped up and down and stretched his arms out, but it was no good. "Humpft," he grumped.

Lily giggled. She could reach the shelf

easily. "Here you go," she said as she passed it down to him. Archie held it

so tightly that a small white cloud of flour puffed up from the bag and settled on his head, turning his hair white. He looked as old as Grandpa! Lily laughed again but Archie scowled.

Uh oh, Lily thought, *Archie's bad mood isn't over yet!* Luckily, Grandma ruffled his hair to brush the flour away, and kissed him on the top of his head. Then, before he could get upset, she read out the next ingredient.

"This is fun," Lily said. "It's just like a treasure hunt!"

Working together, Lily and Archie found cocoa powder – which Grandma said would make the fairy cakes taste chocolatey – caster sugar and butter, and put them all next to the magic jar.

Grandma read out the next ingredient. "Now we need vanilla extract. It's in a tiny bottle. It looks like something a fairy might use!" Grandma laughed as Lily and Archie raced past each other, rushing to get to the larder. Suddenly Lily spotted some teeny bottles, half hidden behind a tin of golden syrup.

"Got it! Vanilla extract!" she cried.

"Well done, Lily." Grandma smiled. "And well done, Archie, too," she added quickly, as his face crumpled.

Grandma had already put a large

mixing bowl on the table next to the scales, with some spoons, a whisk and a sieve.

"What next, Grandma?" Archie asked.

"Now." Grandma clapped her hands. "We're ready to begin!"

3

An Eggy Adventure

"Silly me!" said Grandma as she stared at the baking ingredients laid out on the table. "I almost forgot the eggs." She turned to Archie and Lily. "Lilybee, would you take Archie out to the chicken coop and see if Jessie and Bessie have laid any today?"

Lily started pulling her wellie boots on. She loved Grandma's chickens, and she usually fed them their corn before she went home each evening.

But Archie wasn't putting his wellies on. "We can't go outside," he moaned. "It's raining."

Lily looked out of the window. Raindrops were trickling down the windowpane.

Grandma looked up at a small grey cloud covering the sun. "It's just a little shower. It'll be over in a minute. "

"But I'll get wet," Archie insisted.

"Well, you're not made of sugar," Grandma told him. "You won't melt!"

"Come on, Archie." Lily opened the back door. "We can pretend we're in a *rain*forest. There might be wild animals out there." Lily made her eyes wide and frightened. "Monkeys and lizards and tigers."

"OK!" Archie rushed to the door and quickly put on his raincoat and wellies. Then he dashed outside. "I'm ready first," he told Lily. "That makes me the leader."

Lily didn't mind. At least he wasn't being so grumpy. Grandma stood at the door watching them as they set off towards the chicken coop. "Remember to ask Jessie and Bessie nicely for the eggs," she called after them. "And make sure you say thank you."

They set off down the narrow garden path between the vegetable patch and the strawberry plants, all the time looking out for pretend crocodiles and snakes.

The rain drizzled down, coating the garden in sparkling drops. Archie picked up a long twig and held it like a sword. When they came to the tall rhubarb stalks, he pushed the large leaves aside.

"What can you see?" Lily whispered as Hector stalked past her and rubbed his head against her leg.

"*Tiger!*" Archie shouted. "Run!"

Hector gave a surprised meow and rushed back to the safety of the kitchen as Lily and Archie ran shrieking and laughing towards the chicken coop.

The coop had a triangular shed where Jessie and Bessie slept, and a run covered with wire mesh where they could walk about and scratch at the ground. It was just big enough for Grandma to go in if she bent over, and Lily and Archie fitted inside easily.

Lily opened the door and dashed into the run. Archie left his stick outside and followed Lily. She made sure to close the door after them. They didn't want the chickens escaping or, worse still, tigers getting in.

It was quite dark, but nice and warm, and it smelled of wood and straw. Bessie and Jessie were resting on their nests, sheltering from the rain.

"Hello, girls!" Lily said, just like Grandma always did. "Do you have any eggs for us?"

Bessie clucked softly and stood up. Beneath her was a warm brown egg.

But Jessie stayed snuggled

in her nest. She tilted her head to one side and blinked at Archie. Archie stared at her. "She's not getting up."

"Don't worry," Lily told him. "I know what to do." She reached up to a plastic tub on a shelf above the nests and pulled off the lid. "Let's give them some corn," she told Archie. She scattered a handful of the corn on the floor of the shed. Bessie flew down and started pecking at it, and moments later Jessie stood up and ruffled her feathers.

"Look!" Archie said. He was pointing to a white egg lying in her nest. He stood back as Jessie made a soft clucking sound and flapped down to the floor. While she pecked at the corn, Archie collected the eggs.

"That's one egg from Bessie and one from Jessie," Lily told him. She smiled at her little brother as he carefully picked the eggs up. "How many eggs does that make?"

Archie looked down at his hands. "Two!" he told her.

"Well done, Archie!" Lily cried. "See, you *can* do your numbers!"

She put the tub of grain up on the shelf. "Let's get back to the kitchen. I want to start baking." Then she remembered something.

"Thank you for the eggs," she told the chickens. "We're going to make magical fairy cakes with them!"

Bessie and Jessie clucked again. Lily leaned down to Archie. "Do you know what they said?" she smiled. Archie shook his head, his brown eyes wide. "They said, '*Sounds delicious!*'"

Lily and Archie both laughed as they raced back through the garden. The rain had stopped and the sun was out again. Lily had forgotten all about crocodiles, snakes and tigers. Instead she was imagining the taste of delicious fairy cakes.

Lily reached the back door first. "Come on," she called to Archie, tugging off her wellingtons before hurrying inside. Archie rushed up to the doorway holding the eggs. He kicked off his right boot but when he tried to wriggle his left foot free, Archie lost his balance and started to wobble.

"Oh . . . oh . . . *oh!*" he cried, and fell

over with a bump.

Lily turned round just in time to see Archie burst into tears. He was lying on the ground, and there in his hand was a mess of yolk and shell where an egg used to be.

Mixing Up Some Magic

Grandma came running out into the garden. Lily was still staring at her little brother. In one hand Archie was holding Bessie's brown egg, but the fingers of his other hand were covered in runny gloop and bits of white shell.

"Never mind," Grandma said cheerfully, "it doesn't matter."

Archie's cheeks were pink and his eyes were full of tears. When he spoke his voice shook. "I broke an egg," he sobbed. "We can't make the fairy cakes now."

"There, there, don't worry," Grandma said, passing the smooth brown egg to Lily.

Lily felt like she was about to cry too, as she stared at the egg. She'd wanted to cook magical fairy cakes so much, and now everything was ruined. Feel Good Fairy Cakes had made Archie feel even *worse*!

"Come on, let's wash your hands, Archie," Grandma was saying. Archie cried even harder as Grandma washed the gloopy egg off his fingers.

"Hmmm, it looks like we need the Feel Good Fairy Cakes more than ever," Grandma said thoughtfully.

"But we can't make them now!" Archie wailed.

"Yes we can," Grandma soothed. "We just need to find another egg. There might still be one from yesterday in the fridge. Lily, why don't you go and look?"

Lily ran over to the fridge, her heart beating fast. Before she opened it, she closed her eyes for a second and wished as hard as she could. *Please let there be an egg inside.* She wanted to make Feel Good Fairy cakes so much. She tugged at the fridge door and peered in. There was lots of yummy-looking food, but there were no eggs.

Lily's heart sank. Archie was going to be sadder than ever now that they couldn't make Feel Good Fairy Cakes. She sighed and pulled the door shut. But as she did so something caught her eye. There, on the inside of the door, were two brown eggs!

"Grandma! Archie! Look!" Lily yelled

as she held them up. "Don't worry. There were two eggs in the fridge."

"Phew!" Grandma gave a little smile. "See," she said, giving Archie a hug. "It's OK after all. And we've even got one spare for my breakfast tomorrow. Now go and wash your hands again and then we can start making some cakes!" Archie sniffed and gave a watery smile, then went off to the bathroom.

"While Archie's doing that, I've got a job for you, Lily," Grandma said. "It's called 'creaming' the butter and sugar, but it just means mixing them together."

Lily plopped the soft butter into a bowl while Grandma measured out the right amount of sugar. Then Lily tipped the sugar on top of the butter and started pushing the crunchy crystals into the butter with a fork.

"That's it!" Grandma smiled. "Keep going until it goes white and creamy."

Lily mixed until her arm hurt. "Is it done yet?" she asked Grandma, peering anxiously into the bowl.

"Let's have a look." Grandma whisked the fork through the mixture much more quickly than Lily had done, and soon it started to look creamy and delicious. Lily licked her lips excitedly!

Archie rushed back in and peered into the bowl excitedly. "What can I do?" he asked, as Grandma tied his apron back on.

"Do you want to break the eggs, Archie?" Grandma asked. "In the bowl this time!" Grandma rolled up his sleeves and showed him how to tap the egg against the edge of the bowl until the shell cracked. With Grandma and Lily's help Archie broke both the eggs into the bowl without getting any shell in it.

"Next we add the vanilla essence," Grandma said. "The vanilla makes the fairy cakes extra tasty. Do you want to smell it?"

She opened the bottle and Archie and Lily scrambled over to sniff it. Archie put his nose to the open bottle and breathed in deeply. "Mmmm!" he cried. "It smells like ice cream."

"Can I put it in?" Lily asked. The top of the tiny fairy-sized bottle was a little dropper, and Lily really wanted to play with it.

Grandma gave her the bottle and Lily carefully squeezed the top so that a few drops fell into the bowl.

"Now I have a *very* important job for you, Archie," Grandma said when he'd finished sniffing the vanilla bottle. She handed Archie the sieve. "I need you to shake the flour."

The sieve was made of silver metal with lots of tiny little holes in it. "It looks like a fishing net," Archie said. He held it still while Grandma poured the flour into it. She showed him how to gently shake it from side to side so the flour drifted through.

Then Archie frowned. "Why does it have to go through it?"

"To get rid of all the lumps," Grandma

told him. "You don't want to bite into a lovely chocolatey fairy cake and find a big lump of flour in it, do you?"

Mmmmm. Lily licked her lips. The thought of a tasty fairy cake was already making her tummy rumble!

5

Grump in the Garden

"Can I stir? Can I stir?" Archie jumped up and down.

"Yes," Grandma told him. "We just need to add the cocoa powder to make it chocolatey! Can you measure out two tablespoons?"

Archie peered suspiciously at the brown powder. "It doesn't look like chocolate," he said as he dipped the measuring spoon in. Lily agreed. She was glad they were putting real chocolate chips in too!

"Just you wait until it's all mixed in with the other ingredients," Grandma smiled. "Why don't you hold the bowl still, Lily, and we'll take it in turns to stir."

Once the cocoa powder was added, Lily put her hands on either side of the bowl as Archie's spoon went round and round and all the ingredients turned into a thick chocolatey goo. She could hardly believe that eggs and flour and things turned into something that looked so delicious. It was magical!

"Can we put the chocolate chips in now?" Archie asked excitedly.

Grandma's eyes twinkled. "I think we should treat ourselves to two chips each first, don't you?" she said, opening the pack. "Would you like to count out them out, Archie?"

"I'll help!" Lily offered, but Grandma stopped her.

"Let's see if Archie can do it by himself."

Lily felt cross for a second, but Grandma put her finger to her lips and smiled. Lily realized that Grandma was trying to get Archie to practise his counting. She watched her little brother as he leaned over the chocolate chips.

Archie pushed two chocolate chips towards Grandma and put two in Lily's palm. He counted them out on his fingers. "One . . . two . . . three . . . four." He popped another two into his mouth. "Five . . . six!" he said, giving a big chocolatey grin.

"Well done!" Lily praised him. Grandma gave him a hug.

"Do I get a prize?" Archie asked cheekily.

"Yes, you can have a fairy cake –
when they're cooked!" Grandma joked.
Archie looked longingly at the rest of
the chocolate chips, but he emptied
the packet into the bowl and carried
on stirring.

Lily picked up the recipe from the table and began reading it. "Nearly finished," she smiled. "What next, Grandma?" she asked.

Grandma had her head in a cupboard. "Ah! Here it is!" she cried, putting a tin on the table. It had lots of holes in it, just the right size to fit the cake cases in. "Can you put a case in each of the gaps, Lilybee?" Grandma asked.

Lily popped open the box of cake cases and took out the pretty paper cases. They were a light blue colour and they were covered with tiny little pink spots.

"Make sure you only put one case in each," Grandma told her. "Sometimes they stick together." Lily licked her fingers and rubbed the sides of the cake cases to separate them.

Grandma let Lily spoon the mixture carefully into the cases. Archie helped by telling her which ones needed a bit more in them. Then they both scraped the bowl clean, making sure they got every last bit out. Afterwards, Grandma let them lick their wooden spoons.

"Mmmmm," Lily said, between licks. "I think our Feel Good Fairy Cakes are going to be the best ever."

Archie agreed. "The best in the whole wide world!"

"Meow!" Hector added. He was sitting at Lily's feet, looking up at her hungrily.

"Sorry, Hector, you can't have any," Lily told him. "Chocolate makes cats poorly." Hector gave a small disappointed mew and looked at Archie, but he was busy licking his chocolatey fingers.

"Oh, I'm sure we can find a treat for you too, Hector," Grandma laughed. "We just need to get this in the oven first. Now, the fairy cakes need to bake for twenty minutes."

"Twenty minutes?" Archie wailed. "That's ages!"

Grandma put the pan in the oven and shut the door. "Why don't you go into the garden and play until they're done?"

Lily stared at the oven. She wanted to stay and watch – she'd never seen magical fairy cakes cooking before. Maybe there would be sparkles and fireworks in the oven as the magic baked!

Archie was looking longingly at the oven too. A delicious sweet smell was already starting to come from it.

"The fairy cakes won't cook any faster

if you watch them," Grandma told them. "I'll let you know when they're ready."

Archie gave a grumpy moan as he took his apron off, and plodded over to where his boots were lying at the back door. "I want them to be ready NOW!" he grumbled.

"Come on, Archie," Lily said, reluctantly going outside. "We can go and see if Grandpa's found any more worms."

It was bright and sunny now the rain shower had passed. She could see Grandpa down at the far end of the garden. His hat was bobbing up and down as he dug in the vegetable patch. Hector was busily lapping up fresh rainwater from a small puddle.

Archie sat down on the garden bench and folded his arms. "I'm still not happy," he pouted.

"That's because you haven't eaten

the fairy cakes yet." Lily told him. She picked up a bright red ball lying behind a flowerpot. "Let's play catch."

She threw the ball in a high loop. Archie reached up his hands, but the ball bounced down on his head.

"OW!" Archie said crossly.

"Oops! Sorry!" Lily called, but she couldn't help giggling. Archie looked so cross. Archie kicked the ball grumpily and it flew up, higher and higher – right over the garden fence!

Lily's tummy jumped with worry. Suddenly there was an angry shout from the next-door garden. "Hey! Who did that?" it yelled. Then they heard the heavy thump of feet stomping across the ground towards them.

"Uh oh," Lily whispered. "I think we're in trouble."

6

Baking Magic

Lily and Archie stared in horror as a face peered over the top of the fence. It was Grandma's neighbour, Mr Mellor, and he looked very cross. His grey moustache was twitching and his angry eyes had almost disappeared beneath his thick eyebrows.

"Who threw that ball into my garden?" he frowned down at them. "You should be more careful. It landed on my tulips."

Lily felt her cheeks turn pink. "Sorry, Mr Mellor." She took a deep breath. "We didn't mean to. Please can we have our ball back?"

"No, you can't," he growled. "That way it won't land in my garden again." He disappeared behind the fence still muttering, "Naughty children . . . squashing my tulips."

Archie looked as if he was going to cry. Lily squeezed her little brother's hand, but she was upset too. It was horrible to be shouted at. Archie hadn't sent the ball over the fence on purpose, and she hadn't meant to hit him on the head. Mr Mellor was a big meanie and now he'd made her feel grumpy too. It wasn't fair!

Lily was feeling so cross that she almost told Archie off when he started sniffing. But suddenly she smelt it too. She sniffed the air again and again. There was a delicious smell drifting through the open window!

"The fairy cakes!" Archie whispered.

Lily and Archie rushed to the back door. Lily helped Archie take his wellie boots off this time. Lily could hear Grandma inside, singing along to the radio. They had just made it into the kitchen when the timer went "ding". Lily gave Archie a look of delight and hurried inside. Grandma was already lifting the hot tray out of the oven with her oven gloves.

"Are they ready?" Lily asked.

"Almost," Grandma said, setting the hot tin on the breadboard. "They'll have to cool down before we can eat them. We should start making the topping." She turned round and saw Lily and Archie's miserable faces.

"Oh no, what's wrong now?" she asked.

"Our ball went into Mr Mellor's garden," Lily told her, "and he told us off, even though it was an accident."

"And he won't give it back!" Archie started to cry.

Grandma bent down and wiped the tears from his eyes. "Oh dearie me. I think we need a little feel-good magic right now, don't you?"

Archie sniffed and nodded his head as hard as he could.

Grandma carefully picked up one of the fairy cakes. "They're still too hot to eat," she said, but she unwrapped a small one and broke it in half. She gently blew on the cakes before handing them to Archie and Lily. "But I think you can try these bits."

Lily put the piece of cake in her mouth. Seconds later, warm, soft, fluffy, chocolatey cake spread out on her tongue. It was so delicious she closed her eyes and gave a long happy sigh. "This is *magically* good!" she whispered.

Archie had stopped sniffing. As he bit into his piece of fairy cake his brown eyes grew wide, and his smile grew even wider. Soon he was nibbling it happily.

"Better?" Grandma asked, with a twinkle in her eye.

Archie nodded his head up and down. Just then the microwave pinged.

"Ooh, that's the topping," Grandma

smiled, putting two bowls of melted
chocolate on the table, along with a bowl
of chocolate buttons and some glittery
sprinkles from the Yummy Cupboard.
Lily grinned and
Archie licked his lips
in glee. Their Feel
Good Fairy Cakes
were going to be
beautiful!

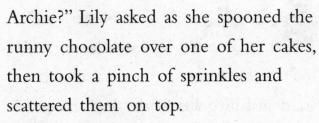

"Now, if we
decorate half the
cakes each, how
many will we have,
Archie?" Lily asked as she spooned the
runny chocolate over one of her cakes,
then took a pinch of sprinkles and
scattered them on top.

"Six!" Archie grinned, as Grandma
retied his apron on for him.

"Well done!" Lily smiled as she looked at her cake. It looked so pretty – almost too nice to eat! Archie was dipping the cakes straight into the chocolate and giggling as he dribbled chocolate all over the table and all over himself. "It's a good thing you're wearing an apron!" Grandma

smiled as she went to make them all a drink.

When she was sure Grandma wasn't looking, Lily dipped the tip of her finger into the smooth melted chocolate.

It tasted just as good as she had expected. Thick and chocolatey and sweet! She glanced back over her shoulder. Grandma was busy helping Archie spoon chocolate on one of his cakes. Lily dipped her finger into the chocolate again. "Mmmm," she said and closed her eyes.

"Lily?" Grandma's voice made her jump. "Have you been eating the melted chocolate?"

Lily opened her eyes. Grandma was standing right next to her. She had her hands on her hips but she didn't look cross.

"How did you know?" Lily gasped.

Grandma winked. "Magic," she said. "And because you're a messy pup. You've got chocolate all round your mouth!"

By the time Grandma had poured them each a glass of milk and made herself a pot of tea in the old brown teapot, Archie had decorated all of his fairy cakes and Lily was just starting her third one, carefully arranging chocolate buttons on the top so they made the shape of a flower. "Please can we eat one now, Grandma?" Archie begged.

"Go on, then," Grandma smiled. Archie grinned and took an enormous bite into his. Lily couldn't resist either, and unpeeled the cake wrapper. The chocolate was still wet and gooey and made a mess over her fingers, but she didn't care! She bit into the cake and felt happiness spread through her. Feel Good Fairy Cakes were delicious!

Just then Grandpa came in from the garden carrying a tub of freshly picked lettuce. "Mmmm, something smells tasty," he said.

"We made Feel Good Fairy Cakes," Lily told him. "They're magic!"

"Oh, really?" Grandpa asked. He washed his hands and sat down in his usual place at the kitchen table. "What's magical about Feel Good Fairy Cakes?" he asked.

"Anyone who eats them is instantly in a good mood!" Lily explained. "And they work! Archie's bad mood has completely gone!"

Archie nodded happily. His mouth was too full of yummy cake to speak.

"In that case, I can't wait to taste them," Grandpa said. "I'm in *ever such* a bad mood," he joked, pulling a horrible grumpy face. Lily and Archie laughed. "Which one can I have?" Grandpa asked. "They all look so delicious!"

"This one!" Archie cried, giving one to Grandpa. "It's got the most chocolate buttons."

Lily watched as he took a bite and slowly chewed it. A smile spread across Grandpa's face.

"Well, Grandma's baking is always good," he said, jumping up to give Grandma a kiss on her cheek. "But this is the best fairy cake I have ever tasted." He looked at his feet. "I think I can feel the magic."

"Can you?" Lily asked. "Really?"

Grandpa nodded. "Yes, my toes are tingling and I can't stop smiling."

"I can't either!" Lily laughed.

"Me neefer!" Archie said with his mouth full of cake. Lily grinned as she looked round at everyone's happy faces. The Feel Good Fairy Cakes had worked their magic, just as Grandma had said they would.

Lily's Idea

Once everyone had eaten a fairy cake,
they sat back happily. Hector purred
loudly as he lapped at a saucer of milk,
and Archie slurped from his own glass so
fast that he got a milk moustache.

"That was so much fun," Lily told
Grandma, once all the cakes were
decorated. "I love baking magical cakes,
and I love eating them even more!" Lily
looked at the recipe lying on the table. It
was dotted with spots and splashes of cake

mixture now. "Can we keep the recipe, Grandma?"

"Of course," Grandma said. "You never know when we might need to make Feel Good Fairy Cakes again. And I've got just the place for you to keep it."

Grandma went into her Yummy Cupboard to search the shelves for something. "Here it is." She carried a beautiful box covered in a lovely flower pattern over to the table and set it down beside Lily. "You can put all your magical recipes in here."

Lily gave Grandma a big "thank you" hug. "Now we can make Feel Good Fairy Cakes whenever we want to!" She put the recipe in the box and Grandma put it up on the shelf next to the jar.

Lily sat down at the table and looked up at the jar happily. Archie was making happy *brrrrrum*ing noises beside her as he ran his toy truck over the tabletop. Grandpa sat in his chair, reading the newspaper.

"I wonder what magical recipe will be in the jar next time?" Lily thought out loud. She couldn't imagine anything tasting better than Feel Good Fairy Cakes.

"Who knows?" Grandma gave a big smile and shrugged her shoulders. "But I'm sure the magic will know *just* the right recipe to give us."

Lily looked thoughtful. "So whenever we need something, the jar will have a recipe for us?"

"Yes! That's cos it's magical, silly!" Archie told her.

Lily gave her little brother a hug. It was so nice that he was back to his usual cheerful self. She wished everyone could be happy all the time.

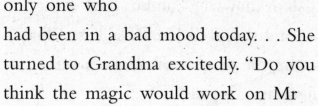

Lily suddenly had an idea. Archie wasn't the only one who had been in a bad mood today. . . She turned to Grandma excitedly. "Do you think the magic would work on Mr

Mellor?" she asked.

"Oh, I would think so," Grandma replied, a smile spreading over her face.

"We should take him a Feel Good Fairy Cake!" Lily cried.

"That's a very nice idea, Lilybee," Grandma said.

Lily didn't really want to visit scary Mr Mellor, but she did want to see if the magic would work on him. She chose the prettiest cake with the most sparkles, and Grandma put it on a plate for her. Lily took a deep breath and held Archie's hand. "Come on, Archie," she said, sounding braver than she felt.

Archie hid behind Lily as they walked next door and rang the doorbell. It wasn't a nice musical bell like Grandma's but a buzzer that sounded like a very loud wasp.

The door opened and Mr Mellor stared
down at them.

"What do you want?" he snapped.
"We're sorry our ball went in your
garden," Lily explained. Archie peered out
from behind her and nodded. Lily was

feeling less brave now that Mr Mellor was glaring at her.

"It wasn't really Archie's fault," Lily explained. "It was the bad mood."

Archie nodded in agreement.

Mr Mellor was still scowling. "Bad mood?" he asked.

"Yes," Lily told him. "Anyway, we brought you this," she said, holding the cake out in front of her. "We made them with Grandma this afternoon. It's a Feel Good Fairy Cake."

"Humpft," Mr Mellor said, taking the fairy cake.

He didn't even say "thank you"! Lily thought to herself.

She and Archie watched as Mr Mellor bit into the cake. He chewed so fast his moustache bounced up and down. But then his eyebrows lifted and his eyes opened wide. "Mmmmm!" he said.

He took
another bite and
then another.
Lily watched him
closely to see if
she could see the
magic working.

"Isn't it
yummy?" Archie
said excitedly, as
Mr Mellor popped
the last piece of
cake in to his mouth.

"Delicious," Mr Mellor mumbled.
"Er. . . Thank you."

His moustache twitched and Lily saw
a small smile curling the corners of
his mouth. It must be the magic! Lily
squeezed Archie's hand. Mr Mellor wiped

the crumbs from his moustache with the napkin and stared at them. "I suppose you want your ball back?"

Lily nodded. "Yes, please."

Mr Mellor disappeared inside the house and Lily and Archie looked at each other. "It worked!" they said together.

Mr Mellor came back and handed the ball to Archie. "Make sure you keep it away from my tulips," he warned.

Mr Mellor still wasn't in a good mood, Lily decided. It would take a *lot* of fairy cakes to do that, but at least he wasn't in *quite* such a bad mood.

Lily skipped all the way back down the garden path. Archie walked beside her, taking giant dinosaur strides. Archie counted his steps all the way back to Grandma's house and didn't make one mistake. "Lily!" he gasped. "I can do my numbers too!"

Lily squeezed his hand as he ran in to tell Grandma.

But the magic wasn't finished yet.

There was a surprise for Archie when they got back to Grandma's. Mum and Dad had arrived to take them home and were sitting at the kitchen table. "Look what I found in the car," Dad said. He held up Archie's lost dinosaur pen. "It must have fallen out of your school bag this morning."

Archie could hardly believe it. "I've had the best day ever!" he yelled.

"And how was your day, Lily?" Mum asked.

Lily looked at the jar, back in its usual place on the dresser shelf and sparkling brightly in a ray of sunshine. She felt her toes start to tingle and an extra big smile

crossed her face.

"It was magical!"

Look out for more

Bake a Wish

books

Bake a Wish
Can-Do Crispies
Includes FANTASTIC cut-out-and-keep recipe card!
Lorna Honeywell

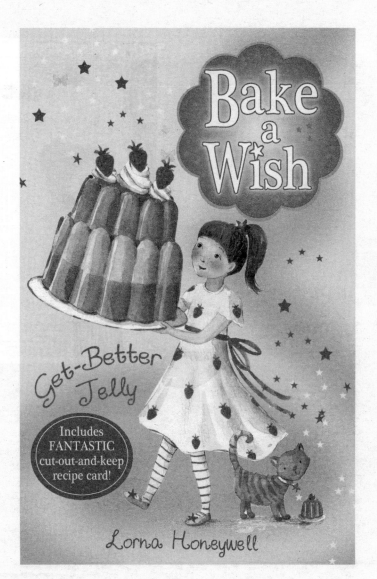

Bake a Wish

Get-Better Jelly

Includes FANTASTIC cut-out-and-keep recipe card!

Lorna Honeywell

Bake a Wish

Feel Fearless Flapjacks

Includes
FANTASTIC
cut-out-and-keep
recipe card!

Lorna Honeywell